For Neil and Leigh—Jen Bryant
For my mother and father, for who they are and what they are—James Browne

Original watercolor illustrations copyright James Browne.

Director of Publications: Susan Randolph
Designer: Suzanne DeMott Gaadt, Gaadt Perspectives, LLC (for Giulia)
Typeface: Filosofia Regular
Printer: Seaber Turner & Associates
Printed in USA

10 9 8 7 6 5 4 3 2 1

      Library of Congress Cataloging-in-Publication Data
Bryant, Jennifer.
 Into Enchanted Woods / by Jen Bryant; illustrated by James Browne.--1st ed.
    p. cm.--(A Winterthur book for children)
Summary: In the Winterthur Museum's gardens, a brother and sister who
have strayed from the path meet an elf named Root, who introduces them
to the magic of the Enchanted Woods.
 ISBN 0-912724-59-5 (Hardcover)
1. Henry Francis du Pont Winterthur Museum (Del.)--Juvenile fiction.
[1. Henry Francis du Pont Winterthur Museum (Del.)--Fiction.
2. Elves--Fiction. 3. Magic--Fiction. 4. Gardens--Fiction.
5. Brothers and sisters--Fiction.] I. Browne, James, 1969- ill.
II. Title. III. Series.
 PZ7.B8393 In 2001
 [Fic]--dc21
          2001001961

Into Enchanted Woods

by Jen Bryant
illustrated by James Browne

A Winterthur Book for Children

Winterthur
An American Country Estate
Winterthur, Delaware 19735

10/21/01

Dear Cleo,
May all your dreams
come true.
Best Wishes!

he afternoon sun spilled
yellow ribbons between the trees
and warmed the shoulders of the two children
who had wandered off the trail
to pick blackberries.

Once in while they stopped to watch
the rabbits crouched below the thicket
or to let a painted turtle pass
or to investigate a nest of busy ants.

"It's getting late," Tara told her younger brother,
who was busy licking the tart juice from his lips.
"We'd better head home."

Thomas plucked a handful of berries
and popped them into his mouth.
"O.K," he said. "But let's come back tomorrow."

They gathered their baskets and began to walk
toward the trail they had followed
from their backyard. But after a few moments,
the narrow path disappeared.

"You know the way, don't you Tara?"
Thomas asked.
"Sure—sure I do," replied Tara, trying to
sound confident.
Mother's words echoed in her head:
Watch out for your brother—Stay on the
trail, and be home in time for dinner.

Tara looked around quickly. She had
a funny feeling—as if someone was
watching. Then she spied
a break in the thicket.
"This way!" she said,
taking Thomas by the hand.

On the other side, they stepped into a clearing
surrounded by blooming bushes. The grass
was thick with daisies and purple violets,
and the air was filled with the whir of wings.
Bees and hummingbirds flitted among the flowers and vines.

Like a lovely dream Tara thought—
and for a moment, she forgot they were lost.

"What's that sound?" asked Thomas.
Tara listened. Somewhere close by,
something was rustling and scraping.
Tara walked slowly to the edge of the clearing.
She pushed back a honeysuckle branch and saw . . .

squatting on a mossy log, a most
unusual creature. His body was smaller than
a dog's, and he was dressed head to toe
in a soft, brown suit. His large ears stuck
out of his hat, pointing toward the sky,
and his dark eyes twinkled like a pair
of polished stones.

When the creature saw them, he slid
down from the log and—to Tara and
Thomas's amazement—came

        skipping and hopping

                sashaying and shuffling

                        whirling and twirling

to greet them.

"Lost your way?"
the little man asked.
Tara began to shake her head,
then instead nodded slowly.

"Well, sort of . . ."
she said cautiously,
gripping Thomas's hand
and backing away.

"Well then, cheer up!"
chirped the little man.
"In losing your usual way,
you have found the
Enchanted Woods.
My name is Root—
I'm the guardian elf of Oak Hill
and the fairies' most trusted
advisor!"

Root removed his hat and
made a slow bow.

"Enchanted Woods? Fairies?" Tara was not sure—
she had never heard of such a place before.

"I thought I saw a fairy when we were
picking berries!" said Thomas,
who was not at all afraid. "She was small and
green and had wings like a dragonfly."

"That would be Glimmer," explained Root.
"She has no doubt flown off to tell the others
of your arrival. You see, we have not had
children here for many years—the fairies will
be so pleased!"

Tara's eyes narrowed as she looked up into the
branches, inspecting them. She walked slowly
around two giant trunks. She lifted a stone.
"Well, I don't see any fairies . . ." she said,
shaking her head.

"Aaahhh, but they see YOU," whispered Root.
"Fairies are everywhere in the Enchanted Woods.
And remember: they may change themselves into
animals, flowers, birds, insects, and even trees . . ."

Just then, the wind rustled the leaves
in the branches of the poplars and a flock
of finches flew over their heads
chirping and twittering. A glittering
green-gold dragonfly zigzagged by,
and another fluttered over a patch of buttercups.

"Follow me!" cried Root

        skipping and hopping,

                sashaying and shuffling,

                        whirling and twirling,

along a brick walk with a snake-shape
twisting down the middle. The path
ended near the foot of a wooden bridge
nestled between two tall trees.

"SSHHHH!!" Root warned the children who
were running along behind, trying to keep up.
"Tiptoe across—we mustn't wake the sleeping troll."

On the other side, a circle of trees surrounded
a wooden pole. A gentle breeze scooped up
leaves and whirled them around and around.

"Look—it's the fairies—they're dancing!" cried Thomas.
Dropping Tara's hand, he ran, giggling, to the center where he
whirled and swirled among the golds and greens until he was too dizzy
to stand and fell down in a grinning heap.

"You're silly!" said Tara,
helping her brother up.
She plucked a leaf from
Thomas's hair, and it
quickly whisked away
on the wind.

"Come on—There's lots to see!" shouted Root as he
skipped and hopped,
sashayed and shuffled,
whirled and twirled
toward a small house in the distance.
The children followed quickly, and soon . . .

the three of them stood together under
the thatched roof of a forest cottage.
Tara's eyes grew wide when she glimpsed the
tiny table and chairs and the smooth stone hearth.
"Who lives here?" she asked Root.

"Well, there are elves and pixies, brownies
and gnomes, fairies and . . ."

"No, no, no—I mean who *really* lives here?"
Tara asked again, still unbelieving.

Root scratched his ear and sighed.
"Elves and pixies, brownies and gnomes,
fairies and . . ."

"OK, OK, OK!" Tara exclaimed, checking
carefully under the chairs and into the corners
for signs of enchanted creatures.

"Hey, Tara—look at me!" called Thomas
from the other side of the table. He sat in one
of the tiny chairs, wiping a wide stripe
of chocolate from his chin.

"Where did you get *that*?" Tara inquired,
inspecting her brother's hands and
sweet-streaked face.

"I was just sitting here wishing I had
something good to eat . . . and then,
just like that, I did!"

Tara looked hard at Thomas. "You brought
that in your pocket, didn't you?"

Thomas said nothing but continued to lick
chocolate from his hands. Tara looked
at Root, who merely shrugged and winked.

"This is all very nice," said Tara,
"but I promised Mother we'd be home for dinner."
Root straightened his cap. "Then we'd best
move along," he said, and together they

       skipped and hopped,

              sashayed and shuffled,

                     whirled and twirled

out of the fairy cottage and onto a long ramp.
Up and up, higher and higher they climbed until they
came to a giant circle of sticks. Thomas jumped into
the center among three enormous eggs.

"Are all enchanted nests this big?" Tara wondered.
Root chuckled. "They come in all sizes—but the fairies
built this one just for children to play in."

They took turns sitting atop the giant eggs
and peering over the edge of the woven nest.

"I'm thirsty," declared Thomas.
"So am I," said Tara.
"Good!" said Root.
"Then you're ready for what comes next."

He sashayed ahead and waited for them beside a squatting frog.
"Repeat after me," Root said:

Water run, water flow, water come, water go!

The children repeated—

Water run, water flow, water come, water go!

A stream of cool, clean water bubbled and gurgled
from the pump. They took turns, pausing to watch
the silvery current splash into an old
trough, then finger its way over a small hill
of stones and odd-shaped blocks.

"A fish! I see a fish!" cried Thomas, wading into
the shallow water. A cloud of dragonflies
hovered over the trough. A bird called. Another
answered. A squirrel skittered shyly by.
Root smiled. "The fairies are pleased you're here."
Tara splashed her hand in the water.
"Yes, but you promised we'd . . ."
"I know, I know," Root interrupted. "Home
for dinner. I didn't forget."

And he

        skipped and hopped,

                sashayed and shuffled,

                        whirled and twirled

along a stone path between a pair of snail-shaped pillars.
"What's THAT?" asked Thomas. "A witch's hat?"
"A giant mushroom?" Tara guessed. Root leaped and hopped excitedly.
"This," he announced, bowing low before them, "is the Tulip Tree House,
my favorite spot. Elves live in hollow trees, you know."
"Do you live here?" Thomas asked.
"Sometimes," Root replied.

Inside it was dark and smelled like bark, but it was not unpleasant.
The children ran their fingertips along the walls.
"Here's a riddle," Root said:
"How many elves does it take to fill the Tulip Tree House?"
Tara thought for a moment. "I don't know."
Thomas shrugged. "Me neither."

Root whirled and twirled. He loved riddles.
"About 95 the last time we tried—but then it rained,
and we fit 96! Our ears shrink a little when they're wet."

They followed their friend to a circle of tall pillars. Tara hid behind one—
Thomas found her. Thomas hid behind another—Tara found him.
"My turn!" said Root. But neither Tara nor Thomas
could find him. Tara put her hands on her hips
and cried out, "No fair using magic!"
"Oh all right, picky picky!" said Root,
sliding down from his perch atop the nearest pillar.

"Hey, how'd you get up there?" cried Thomas.
Root just winked. "Care for some tea?" he asked.
The three sat in the center of the circle and sipped enchanted tea
from acorn cups. Overhead, a gang of squirrels chittered and scolded.

As soon as the tea was gone, they found themselves standing among a strange
arrangement of stones scattered in a spiral shape in a nearby clearing.

"What an odd spot," remarked Tara.
"I like it!" exclaimed Thomas, leaping to the top of a flat rock to inspect the view.
"It looks like my box of favorite things—the one I keep under my bed at home."
Tara rolled her eyes. "You mean your junk box."
"It's NOT junk," Thomas insisted. It's just special stuff I found, that's all."

Root scooted under a large arch and twirled over the top of another. "Fairies collect things, too," he said, spreading his arms out wide. "They have gathered these Story Stones from all over Oak Hill—each one has its own tale to tell."

Root pointed to a smooth, round boulder. "That one will tell you all the secrets of water— how it flows and carries fish, how when it freezes, children skate on the ice, and when the ice melts, how it feeds the trees and flowers and glistens like silver in the sun."

"Tell us about this one," demanded Thomas, jumping over to a piece of slate shaped like a table. "Once there were two wonderful children who wandered into the Enchanted Woods," said Root, somewhat sadly. "They met a special friend who wanted them to stay— but he promised to help them get home..." "In time for dinner," added Tara.

Thomas frowned. "Is there more to see?"
Root nodded. He skipped and did a slow sashay.

They followed a path through a thicket of bright, blooming bushes and came
to a patch of mossy ground. "A face!" Thomas exclaimed, looking down.

Tara paced around the small mounds that pushed up from the dirt.
"I think it's a man—a big green man,"
she said and reached down to
tickle his nose.

A sudden breeze
scuttled leaves
across the
clearing. Bees
flew out of the
bushes.

"Bless you!" said
Root to the
Green Man.

"Bet you can't find me!" came Thomas's voice from somewhere nearby.
"Bet I can," answered Tara, inspecting a neat ring of toadstools.
She stepped inside the circle . . .

WHOOOSH! Fountains of cool mist spurted up. "Hey, wait for me!"
Thomas slipped out from behind the big oak bench where he'd been hiding.
He hopped into the circle and was soon as damp as his sister.
When the water stopped, they

    skipped and hopped,

        sashayed and shuffled,

           whirled and twirled

along a flat stone path until they were dry.

Glancing down, they noticed the
stones made a swirling pattern.
"Like a puzzle for our feet," said Thomas.
And he and Tara began to follow it.
They were so busy trying to find the end,
they didn't notice that Root had
disappeared.

© J.BROWNE '01

At the last stone, Tara nearly stumbled over a large, brown rabbit who was grazing peacefully in the soft grass.

"Where's Root?" Thomas asked, looking all around. "He can't leave us now—"
"Don't worry," whispered Tara, so as not to scare the rabbit. "He won't break his promise."
She watched the creature closely for a moment. It was larger than most rabbits, and something about it seemed familiar.

The rabbit stopped eating and began hopping toward the thicket. Tara grabbed Thomas's hand. "C'mon!"

A narrow path led them through thick brush.
Sure enough, on the opposite side, the thicket
opened up to a view they knew well.
"I told you he wouldn't break his promise,"
said Tara to Thomas, who was already running
past the swing set toward their house.

Tara stood still for a moment. A blue-green dragonfly
fluttered by. A flock of finches twittered loudly
in a tree. The rabbit sat below a berry bush,
twitching his pointed ears.
He winked, then disappeared.

The Real Enchanted woods

Enchanted Woods was funded through the generosity of interested donors and friends, through the leadership and support of the entire Lois F. and Henry S. McNeil family.

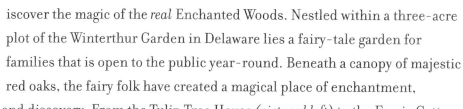

Discover the magic of the *real* Enchanted Woods. Nestled within a three-acre plot of the Winterthur Garden in Delaware lies a fairy-tale garden for families that is open to the public year-round. Beneath a canopy of majestic red oaks, the fairy folk have created a magical place of enchantment, mystery, and discovery. From the Tulip Tree House *(pictured left)* to the Faerie Cottage, the young (and the young at heart) will find a new world to explore.

Enchanted Woods is located within the larger 60-acre garden at Winterthur, the former country estate of Henry Francis du Pont (1880–1969). An avid horticulturist, du Pont worked with his staff and others to design the world-renowned garden. He selected the choicest plants from around the globe and arranged them in lyrical color combinations, carefully orchestrating a succession of bloom from January to December.

Du Pont was also a passionate collector of early American antiques, which are now displayed in 175 period rooms as well as exhibition galleries. Winterthur offers a variety of tours, exhibitions, and programs for all ages to enjoy.

Winterthur is nestled in the heart of Delaware's beautiful Brandywine Valley, halfway between New York City and Washington, D.C., and close to Philadelphia. For directions and information, please call 800.448.3883, TTY 302.888.4907, or visit Winterthur's web site at www.winterthur.org.